Snapdragon

and
the Odyssey of Élan

J. H. Sweet

Illustrated by Holly Sierra

SOURCEBOOKS
Jabberwocky
AN IMPRINT OF SOURCEBOOKS

Published by Sourcebooks Jabberwocky, an imprint of Sourcebooks, Inc.
P.O. Box 4410, Naperville, Illinois 60567–4410
(630) 961–3900
Fax: (630) 961–2168
www.jabberwockykids.com

Library of Congress Cataloging-in-Publication Data

Sweet, J. H.
    Snapdragon and the odyssey of Élan / J. H. Sweet ; illustrated by Holly Sierra.
       p. cm.
    Summary: Because of their proven problem solving abilities, the fairies
Snapdragon and Dove are chosen to help Élan the dragon pass the important
Rites of Dragondom.
    [1. Fairies—Fiction. 2. Dragons—Fiction. 3. Monsters—Fiction. 4. Problem
solving—Fiction.] I. Sierra, Holly, ill. II. Title.
    PZ7.S9547Sn 2009
    [Fic]—dc22
                              2008035262

                        Printed and bound in China.
                    OGP 10 9 8 7 6 5 4 3 2 1

To Dave and Clarann,
and to a peaceful journey through life

MEET THE

Snapdragon

NAME:
Bettina Gregory

FAIRY NAME AND SPIRIT:
Snapdragon

WAND:
Spiral-Shaped Black
Boar Bristle

GIFT:
Fierceness and speed

MENTOR:
Mrs. Renquist,
Madam Swallowtail

FAIRY TEAM

Dove

NAME:
Elise Reynolds

FAIRY NAME AND SPIRIT:
Dove

WAND:
Small Piece of
Green Bamboo

GIFT:
Ability to inspire peace
and settle conflicts

MENTOR:
Mrs. Pelter,
Madam June Beetle

Madam Swallowtail

NAME:
Mrs. Renquist

FAIRY NAME AND SPIRIT:
Madam Swallowtail

WAND:
White Clover Blossom

GIFT:
Strength and endurance

MENTOR TO:
Primrose and Snapdragon

Inside you is the power to do anything™

Marigold and the Feather of Hope, the Journey Begins
Dragonfly and the Web of Dreams
Thistle and the Shell of Laughter
Firefly and the Quest of the Black Squirrel
Spiderwort and the Princess of Haiku
Periwinkle and the Cave of Courage
Cinnabar and the Island of Shadows
Mimosa and the River of Wisdom
Primrose and the Magic Snowglobe
Luna and the Well of Secrets
Dewberry and the Lost Chest of Paragon
Moonflower and the Pearl of Paramour
Snapdragon and the Odyssey of Élan

Come visit us at fairychronicles.com

Contents

Chapter One

Spring Break

Spring break from school was supposed to be restful and relaxing. Unfortunately, for Bettina Gregory, spring break was one of the busiest weeks of year. The first weekend had been somewhat quiet. Bettina had spent most of it reading, cleaning her room, and helping her mother in the garden. First, they uncovered iris and daffodil bulbs that had been protected with mulch for the winter. Then they planted several new bushes.

On Monday, Bettina met up with several of her friends and her Girls Club sponsor,

Mrs. Renquist. Together, they cleaned up a two-mile stretch of country highway that their Girls Club Chapter had adopted for regular litter clean up.

Bettina was happy to help keep the roads clean in her area, though it was hard to believe that some people still littered. She couldn't understand why others weren't as proud as she was to live in such a beautiful place, and why road trashers didn't have more respect for the earth. The types of things the girls were picking up were obviously not blown-away trash items. Most of the junk had been thrown out of car windows or deliberately dumped.

Having been thoroughly tired out by the highway clean up venture, Bettina was looking forward to slightly less strenuous activities for the rest of the week. Little did she know that she was going to be in for an exciting and extremely active adventure.

Beginning Tuesday, Mrs. Renquist had arranged for Bettina to have a two-night sleepover with one of her friends, Hope Valdez, at Mrs. Renquist's house. On Wednesday morning, the girls would be attending a special celebration called Fairy Circle.

In addition to being just like other young girls, Bettina and Hope were also fairies, and had been given unique fairy spirits. Fairies were tasked with the job of protecting nature and fixing problems, so Bettina and many of her friends stayed extremely busy with fairy activities all year long.

Bettina was blessed with a snapdragon fairy spirit. As a fairy, Snapdragon wore an orange and yellow dress made of furled snapdragon petals that came to just above her knees. She also had tall, wispy orange wings and short, curly, light brown hair. In the belt of her dress, she carried a small pouch of pixie dust, the fairy handbook, and her wand.

Fairy wands came in many different varieties. They could be made from almost any object and were bewitched to help fairies perform magic. Snapdragon's wand was a black boar bristle that was spiraled like a corkscrew.

Each fairy was given a unique gift that was like a strength or specialty. Snapdragon's special fairy gift included fierceness and speed. The snapdragon flower was named because the mouth of the flower resembled the mouth of a dragon, and Snapdragon's fairy gift came from this likeness. She could fiercely defend against attack, if necessary; and she could fly very fast, just like a speedy dragon.

Hope was a luna moth fairy. In fairy form, she had glowing, pale green wings and wore a shimmering, soft green dress.

Luna carried a prickly pear cactus thorn wand, but she never used it because her special fairy gift was the ability to perform magic without a wand. She also had amazingly keen eyesight.

Each young fairy was assigned a mentor to act as a teacher and supervisor. Mentors guided young fairies' actions to help them learn how to use their powers properly.

Mrs. Renquist was a swallowtail butterfly fairy and acted as Snapdragon's mentor. Madam Swallowtail had magnificent black wings with ivory eyespots. She wore a satiny black dress and carried a white clover blossom wand that looked like a tiny fireworks explosion. Madam Swallowtail's special fairy gift involved strength and endurance. This gift was common to all butterfly and moth fairies.

Luna's mentor was Mrs. Thompson, a finch fairy. Madam Finch was also a Girls Club sponsor. She too was staying with

Madam Swallowtail for a few days while her house was being painted.

On the first night of the sleepover, both Luna and Snapdragon talked excitedly about their special Fairy Circle meeting scheduled for the next day. Luna had received a nut message over the weekend from another fairy friend, Primrose. Nut messages were hollowed-out nuts that fairies used to send notes and letters to one another. Birds and animals usually delivered the messages.

Primrose had heard a rumor that a very unique new fairy would be joining their group—a snake fairy. None of the fairies had ever met a snake fairy before. Even though their fairy group included a toad fairy and a chameleon fairy, the girls were surprised to learn of the existence of a snake fairy. For some reason, snakes didn't seem very fairylike. Luna and Snapdragon were still speculating over this when Madam Swallowtail and Madam Finch came into the bedroom to tell the girls it was time to get to sleep.

Snapdragon and Luna begged their mentors to tell them about the snake fairy. Madam Swallowtail agreed to tell them a little, but only a limited amount because Madam Toad herself wanted to explain a few things about the new fairy.

Madam Toad was the leader of the Southwest region of fairies. She was a very old and wise fairy, and always made the careful selection of which fairies would go on specific fairy missions. Her decisions were usually based on certain fairy gifts and combinations of fairies to form a powerful team. The fact that all of the fairies were different was what gave them strength as a group. Under Madam Toad's careful guidance, the fairies of the Southwest region had never failed on a mission.

Madam Swallowtail informed Snapdragon and Luna that the new fairy had been given the fairy spirit of a harlequin snake. And as far as anyone knew, Harlequin was the only snake fairy in existence, anywhere.

Madam Toad would be informing everyone of the details of the new addition to the group at Fairy Circle because she needed to explain several things about Harlequin's unique fairy spirit and her abilities.

That was all Madam Swallowtail would share with Snapdragon and Luna, despite their persistent pleadings. But it was enough for the girls to whisper excitedly back and forth for nearly an hour, wondering about their new fairy friend.

Chapter Two

Fairy Circle

The location for Fairy Circle was very unusual this time. Normally, the fairies met out in the woods, or in secluded parks, under trees that had special meaning. The fairies had met under a sycamore tree when they needed to recharge the Cave of Courage because sycamore trees were thought to represent strength and courage. Most recently, the group had met under an apricot tree when their mission involved seeking out Paramour, the Goddess of Love, because apricot trees were considered to be symbolic of love.

Today, the Fairy Circle meeting was taking place in an abandoned rock quarry. Many area quarries were recycled into something else when they were no longer used to harvest rock and gravel. Sometimes, old quarries were made into amusement parks, golf courses, and nature parks. However, this quarry had not yet taken on a new identity. A few scrubby mesquite and chinaberry trees had managed to take root in the rocky sides and bottom of the massive hole, along with several other types of bushes and plants, but there were no larger trees.

The fairies gathered under a tiny chinaberry tree that had just started budding for spring. It had already lost all of its golden berries of winter. Many of the berries were lying scattered on the ground, and some of the girls made a game out of kicking them around like soccer balls and playing toss with them. The small chinaberry tree

provided a limited amount of filtered shade and some seclusion.

Even though the fairies were not meeting under a tree that was specific to the purpose of their gathering, Madam Toad had chosen this site very carefully. They needed privacy and a lot of room for a very special guest arriving later.

Snapdragon and Luna both made their way around the group, visiting with many of their friends, and they stopped to talk to Primrose and her cousin, Hollyhock.

Hollyhock was the only deaf fairy in the region. And most of the fairies were learning American Sign Language so that they could communicate more easily with her. Snapdragon had been studying extra hard to learn many new words and phrases, and she was anxious to see if she was making progress.

Hollyhock thought that some of the hubbub over the rest of the fairies learning sign language was a little silly. She had been able to read lips very well for many years; therefore, most of the fairies did not even need to use sign language to speak to her. However, she appreciated their efforts and didn't comment on this. The only time she really needed an interpreter was for their group discussions when she couldn't get close enough to see everyone's mouths clearly. Since both Primrose and Madam Swallowtail were fluent in sign language, she was always able to participate fully in Fairy Circle meetings.

A lot of speculating was going on about Harlequin, and the possible reason for the strange meeting site. Harlequin was due to arrive later with her mentor, Madam Monarch, and another young fairy named Marigold who was Madam Monarch's niece.

No one could figure out the reason they were meeting in a very large hole in the ground. Primrose, the fairy best able to solve mysteries, did come up with the idea that it must have something to do with size. When this idea was presented, the fairies got very excited to think that maybe a giant or an ogre was going to be their guest today.

As Snapdragon and Luna continued to make their way around the circle, visiting with many of their friends, they stopped to talk to Thistle, who was bragging about her little sister, Emily. Emily was not quite a year old and had also been given a fairy spirit—that of a buttercup flower. Buttercup would not learn that she was a fairy for several years, but Thistle couldn't resist telling her friends, "Emily is already looking like a buttercup." She proudly passed around a picture of a laughing toddler with golden, buttery curls and creamy pink cheeks. The other fairies had to admit that Emily did very much resemble a buttercup flower.

Dusty, whose spirit was that of a dusty-wing skipper butterfly, was happily passing out friendship bracelets that she had been working on very hard since Christmas. She had finally made enough for everyone in the group.

Dusty carefully kept two bracelets in her pocket for Harlequin and Marigold when they arrived. She had made Marigold's bracelet orange and yellow, like marigold flowers. Harlequin's was many different bright colors because when Dusty looked up harlequin snakes in the encyclopedia, she had discovered that they were multi-colored.

The fairies all enjoyed refreshments of scrumptious powdered sugar puff pastries, raspberries, peanut butter and marshmallow crème sandwiches, lemon jellybeans, and homemade fudge. And they had root beer, pomegranate juice, and iced tea to drink.

The fairies were all enjoying the sweets and visiting happily when Madam Toad called the meeting to order. "Welcome, welcome! The first thing we are going to talk about is our newest fairy."

Everyone held their breath and waited, listening carefully. Primrose was interpreting for Hollyhock. Both were as excited as everyone else about the new fairy. Primrose was leaning toward Madam Toad, her ears tuned in to Madam Toad's slightest breath; and Hollyhock was leaning toward Primrose, her eyes listening as hard as they could to Primrose's slightest gesture and the mouthing of Madam Toad's words.

Since all attention was immediately focused on her, Madam Toad smiled and went on. "Madam Monarch is one of our most experienced mentors, so I have chosen her to be Harlequin's mentor. Some of you may have already heard that this is the only fairy, as far as we know, given a snake fairy spirit. Harlequin is also the Fairy of Jokes and Mischief. Her spirit is very similar to brownie fairy spirits." (Brownies were boy fairies, full of mischief.) "And she has many brownie qualities," added Madam Toad. "For one thing, she does not have wings and cannot fly."

The young fairies all looked at one another in surprise. As far as they knew, all fairies had wings and could fly. They had never heard of one that couldn't. Of course, brownies couldn't fly because they didn't have wings. Brownies usually rode on birds and animals to travel.

After this first bit of unusual information had a chance to sink in, Madam Toad continued. "We don't know if the lack of wings and flight is due to her likeness to brownie spirits or the fairy spirit coming from a snake. It doesn't make sense that the reason be based on her snake spirit since Madam Chameleon and I can both fly. Obviously, lizard and amphibian fairies are capable of flight. But because she is the only snake fairy, and there are quite a few toad, salamander, and chameleon fairies, the snake aspect *may* have something to do with it.

"If Harlequin is ever chosen to go on a fairy mission," Madam Toad added, "other fairies will need to watch her closely for safety reasons. Some of you may be needed to help scoop her up out of harm's way if danger presents itself. You may want to practice flying in threes with Harlequin, while holding her hands to lift her. She is able to ride on animals and birds, so most of her traveling will be done in that way. However, she may still need your help sometimes."

Madam Toad paused and thought carefully about what she was going to say next. "Because Harlequin is the Fairy of Jokes and Mischief, she will probably play tricks and pranks like brownies do. Sometimes this may seem bothersome, and might be frustrating if overdone. But we all know that brownies, though full of mischief, are never dangerous. In fact, they are very helpful and have proven themselves as loyal fairy allies. They are also very responsible when it comes to matters of real importance.

"Please do not let a few jokes and a bit of mischief cause you to shun our new friend," Madam Toad stressed. "We must accept her for who she is. Madam Monarch will be keeping a close eye on Harlequin to curb any extreme foolish-ness. But a few tricks here and there should be accepted as normal since they are part of her nature. If we tried to change this, it would be like asking Thistle not to laugh."

The fairies all looked at Thistle in surprise. She was by far the most good-natured fairy in their group, full of laughter and prone to frequent fits of giggles. It would indeed be very strange if Thistle suddenly stopped laughing.

"Finally, we come to her special gift," added Madam Toad. "Harlequin snakes are very much like chameleon lizards. Their colors and markings serve to camouflage them. They are often able to blend in perfectly with their backgrounds. We are all aware of how well Madam Chameleon can disappear into her surroundings. However, Harlequin can actually go one step beyond that because she can become invisible."

Madam Toad had to pause again because several of the fairies gasped in surprise and started murmuring amongst themselves. This was totally unexpected, and even more of a surprise than the fact that Harlequin was a flight-less fairy.

When the noise died down, Madam Toad was able to go on. "Harlequin will be held accountable for the responsible use of her fairy gift, just as all of you are held responsible for not abusing your power or using fairy magic unwisely. I do not believe she will use invisibility to anyone's harm. So far, she has proven herself very trustworthy with regard to her abilities, and she is as anxious as any of you to get on with the fairy business of fixing problems and protecting nature."

Madam Toad had just finished telling them about Harlequin, when Madam Monarch, Marigold, and Harlequin arrived.

Harlequin had straight red hair that was so long it came down to the middle of her back. She had dark, sparkling gray eyes and wore a silky dress that looked a

little like a jester or clown outfit. The dress had a white background with a pattern of many different-colored diamond shapes across the bodice and skirt.

Harlequin carried a cinnamon stick wand that smelled wonderful. Several of the fairies were thinking that if Harlequin suddenly turned invisible, they would probably still be able to smell her wand. And they wondered if a fragrant wand was purposely assigned to their new friend, so that others could be warned of her nearness.

Thistle was especially glad to meet Harlequin because she absolutely loved brownie mischief.

Harlequin was smiling happily, and Madam Toad allowed a short break in their meeting so that the other fairies could introduce themselves and welcome their new friend. However, the break didn't last long because Luna's excellent eyesight spotted the special guest for the day, far off in the distant sky. Her mouth dropped open and she nudged Snapdragon, pointing.

Several other fairies also caught sight of the approaching visitor, and many of them began jumping up and down while clapping their hands. When Teasel and Pumpkinwing shrieked with delight, everyone's attention was drawn to the guest's arrival.

Chapter Three

Elan the Peaceful Dragon

one of the younger fairies had ever seen a dragon before. He circled the quarry several times before landing near the chinaberry tree. Larger than a school bus with his wings folded, the visiting dragon seemed like a small mountain next to the six-inch fairies.

At first, Madam Toad was not able to introduce the guest due to the uproar. Since the fairies were so excited, they were basically out of control. There had been many types of visitors to Fairy Circle in the past including elves, brownies, dwarves, gargoyles, leprechauns, trolls, and gremlins; but there had never been a visitor this exciting before.

Many of the fairies were jumping up and down and hugging each other. Some were giggling and clapping their hands. And a few were looking up dragons in their fairy handbooks. This is the information that the handbooks shared:

Dragons: Dragons are fantastic reptilian monsters with huge wings, sharp claws, and crested heads. Dragons are born of fire and breathe fire. They are magical creatures under the guardianship of Mother Nature, but they are not very numerous. There are very few dragon colonies left in the world because dragons need a lot of space and cannot live too near humans. Dragons have powerful and secret magic, and it is unknown exactly what is included in their magical abilities. However, it is known that dragons have healing powers, absolute honesty, and beyond-this-world fierceness. Dragons do not usually harm fairies, and they normally stay far away from regular human beings. When they do befriend other creatures, their loyalty is extreme, and legendary. Fewer dragons exist today than in the days of old. However, dragons are still being born. Mother dragons lay their eggs in the center of the earth, which is the only place hot enough to hatch dragon eggs. Baby dragons are born in the earth's core and are delivered to the world when they are spewed out of volcanoes on great fountains of fire or plumes of spouting lava.

The visiting dragon was a speckled, fluorescent green and orange color all over with some black streaking on his back. His claws were black, and his eyes were bright blue. He also had a large orange crest on his head that looked like a spiky fin.

Amidst all of the squeals and chatter of the tiny fairies, the dragon waited patiently to be introduced; and he was a little embarrassed by their exuberance. He turned his head from side to side as he demurely closed his eyes. And his green and orange color deepened a bit and took on a hot pink tinge as he blushed at the attention of the fairies.

Finally, Madam Toad had to interrupt the giggles, whispers, and clapping. "Everyone! Everyone! This is Élan. He has traveled far today from one of the dragon colonies to meet with us and ask for our help. Please, quiet down a bit so that we can hear his story."

The fairies finally calmed themselves, and Élan crouched down to address them. Smiling at the fairies with his razor sharp, brilliant white teeth, he began to speak. For such a large creature, Élan was very soft spoken. His voice was gentle and low, and sounded like a warm breeze. "Hello," he said. "I am so glad to be here today. I need your help to accomplish a very important series of tasks.

"I am a young dragon, only two hundred years old. In order to pass into adult dragonhood, I must complete the Rites of Dragondom so that I can earn the respect of my fellow dragons and secure my place in the dragon realm. The Rites of Dragondom is basically a coming of age, ceremonial ritual that all dragons must participate in.

"The quest I have to complete involves facing off with four dangerous monsters. I must overcome each of them to pass on to the next stage of my journey. However, instead of fighting them, I would like to get their permission to pass." Élan paused for a moment before going on. "I hope you understand that some of the stereotypes about dragons are not true. Not all dragons are vicious and dangerous. In fact, many dragons, including myself, are peaceful and would never hurt other creatures intentionally. It is true that we are territorial, but we have to be." With this, Élan outstretched his massive wings. The span was immense, about as wide as a circus tent.

"You can see that dragons need a lot of room," Élan added. "And I can do dragonish things, like fighting, if I need to; but essentially, I am peaceful and wish to coexist in harmony with my fellow creatures." A small hiss of steam came out of Élan's nostrils as he said this.

"My odyssey involves a quest to obtain a fabulous jewel for my queen. I must get past the four monsters, obtain the jewel, and return with it to Queen Elektra; and I have to complete this journey all in one day. The path of the quest is very wide-spread, covering much distance. But that is not a problem. Dragons are very fast flyers and can circle the earth easily in less than a day if needed."

Élan's face wore a slightly troubled frown as he continued. "The problem is that I do not want to hurt any of the creatures I must face. They are terrible foes, and many dragons would likely just plow them down. Dragons can be tremendously fierce, and we possess incredible combat skills, including extremely powerful and secret magic.

"But it is against my nature to harm others. I need to successfully complete my challenge, but I must somehow find a way to do it without hurting others so that I can still live with myself afterwards.

For me, the journey is not as simple as obtaining the jewel for my queen. That would actually be quite an easy task. With force, it would be easy for any dragon to just take what he wants. This is more a test of my true character. And I want to do what is right, rather than what is easy."

Élan's sharp teeth gleamed in the sunlight as he smiled at the fairies and added, "I am appealing to fairies because I know that you are specialists in solving problems. And the fairies in this particular region are almost legendary. Your skills are very highly thought of. Many creatures in many widespread lands know of your triumphs. Stories are told about the fairies of this area: of your frequent successes in helping other magical creatures solve terrible problems."

Many of the fairies were looking at each other in surprise. None of them had ever thought that there would be stories told about them among other magical creatures. And most of them had no idea that their adventures were known to anyone outside of the immediate scope of those involved in any given mission.

Élan finished by telling them, "If there is any way I can complete my quest without fighting, by some peaceful means, I very much want to. It is important to me that I stay true to my character."

By now, with the excitement of meeting Élan, most of the fairies had forgotten that there was a fairy among them capable of brownielike mischief such as playing tricks and pulling pranks. Morning Glory and Firefly were very surprised when several tiny poppy seeds pinged against the backs of their heads.

The seeds didn't hurt, but it was a bit unsettling to have them bounce off their heads. When they turned to look for the source of the assault, Harlequin had already secreted her tiny seed-shooter

straw in the belt of her dress. She looked up, and away, nonchalantly as Firefly and Morning Glory peered at her suspiciously.

But both girls smiled as they again focused their attention on the dragon. If this was about the size of what Harlequin could devilishly dish out, they were not going to get too upset.

Next, Madam Toad made the announcement of who would be chosen to participate in this fairy adventure. "I have decided that Snapdragon will lead this mission," she said. "Dove will accompany her, and Madam Swallowtail will supervise."

Though none of the fairies would have questioned her, Madam Toad explained the reasons for her choices. "Since Snapdragon possesses many dragonish qualities, she will be a great asset to Élan on his journey. And Dove is our Fairy of Peace, so she may also be invaluable to help figure out peaceful solutions to stressful conflict situations."

Thistle was wishing very hard that she had been chosen to go on this mission. But she knew that although she had fierceness, she did not have the speed of Snapdragon. Likewise, Dragonfly was also wishing that she could go, since she was very speedy. However, she knew that she was not as fierce as Snapdragon.

Snapdragon had both fierceness and fastness, and was the best fairy to lead this mission. The fairies respected Madam Toad's decision. She always selected mission participants with great care and wisdom. And the strengths of the selected group were always a perfect combination to form a powerful team for their specific purpose.

Dove joined Snapdragon and Madam Swallowtail, as many of the fairies wished them luck and got ready to leave.

Snapdragon and Madam Swallowtail had not yet had a chance to get know Dove since she had only recently joined their group. They visited with her for a while as Madam Toad and Madam Rose packed up provisions for their trip.

Dove's name was Elise Reynolds, and she had shoulder-length, straight brown hair, pulled back into a French braid. Her fairy spirit was that of a Spanish dove, and her dress was made of tiny, furry, pinkish-gray dove feathers. She also had large feathery wings and carried a small piece of green bamboo for her wand. Dove's special fairy gift was the ability to inspire peace and figure out peaceful solutions to problems. She could also instill pleasant dreams in others because good dreams were often delivered to mankind on the wings of doves.

Madam June Beetle was Dove's mentor, and had previously arranged for

Dove to be on a camping trip for three days with two other young fairies so that Dove could participate in this fairy mission. Madam June Beetle was supervising the camping trip, which also included Periwinkle and Cinnabar. The three of them would anxiously await Dove's return to their campsite at the state park.

As Madam Swallowtail went to have a final word with Madam Toad, Snapdragon discovered a few more things about Dove. Her father was in the military, and her mother was Japanese. Dove lived and attended school in a neighboring city that was only about five miles down the road.

"Wow!" exclaimed Snapdragon, wide-eyed, marveling at her new friend. "You might be one of the most diverse fairies of all time. Since your spirit is that of a Spanish dove, and your mom is Japanese, and your dad is originally from Utah, *and* your hair is French braided—you are probably the most international fairy that ever lived."

Dove was laughing at Snapdragon's observations, especially the part about the French-braided hair. Smiling, she added, "*And* I have a German shepherd." Both girls laughed merrily at this.

Small backpacks had been readied for the fairies and included water, peanut butter and marshmallow crème sandwiches, raspberries, and lemon jellybeans. Since it was still morning, the mission would likely be completed before bedtime, so the fairies would not need blankets and pillows.

Just as they were getting ready to leave, Snapdragon noticed a small white box tied with a fancy red ribbon sitting by her feet. She looked questioningly at Madam Swallowtail and Dove, who both shrugged and shook their heads. Neither of them knew anything about the box, and had not seen anyone place it there.

As Snapdragon untied the ribbon and lifted the lid, a springy, multi-colored toy snake popped out of the box. Though she was startled, Snapdragon was not frightened. Then she heard laughter from a distance in the quarry.

In the process of leaving, Harlequin had turned to watch her gift being opened. Madam Monarch and Marigold were laughing too.

Snapdragon waved at Harlequin. She wasn't at all bothered by the prank; in fact, she thought it was rather funny. She quickly tucked the parti-colored snake back into its box and slipped the gift into her backpack. Then the three fairies approached Élan.

Chapter Four

The Hydra

"I think it will be best if you ride on my head," said Élan, as the fairies hovered in front of him. "I can use dragon magic to protect you from the wind, but it will not work in my wing area or across my back because that is where my speed comes from. We will be flying very high and very fast, so you will need to hold onto my crest."

Snapdragon flew up immediately and settled herself into the crook between the first and second spikes of Élan's horny crest. The fin-like crest had five spikes, so there was room for Dove and Madam

Swallowtail to sit behind Snapdragon in two of the other dips. So far, this was great fun for the fairies. It was like riding a horse, but an extremely gigantic horse with scales, claws, wings, sharp teeth, and fire.

As Élan rose out of the quarry with slow, rhythmic flaps of his enormous wings, he clicked together two claws on his right front foot, like he was snapping. As a tiny purple spark appeared near his nose, an immediate stillness settled around his head, completely covering the fairies. They felt as though they were inside of a protective glass bubble. Though the dragon was picking up height and speed, and the ground far below was starting to look blurred, the fairies felt no breeze or wind of any kind.

As they rose ever higher above the clouds, Snapdragon asked, "Are we going to the dragon colony first?"

"No," answered Élan. "We will proceed directly to the first obstacle. I cannot return to the colony without the jewel for Queen Elektra."

"Where is your home?" asked Dove.

"I'm sorry, but I can't tell you," answered Élan. "Dragons are not allowed to reveal the locations of dragon colonies to humans. I *can* tell you that there are four dragon colonies left in the world. But none of them are on the North American Continent."

A few seconds later, Élan announced, "We are over Mexico now." The fairies were very surprised at the speed of the dragon. They had been in South-Central Texas only a few minutes before, but because the air around Élan's head was very still, they had no idea how fast they were traveling.

"We need to make a short detour," Élan said, grinning. "I'm afraid I can't resist."

The dragon swooped low over the mountainous, forested landscape. And Élan was so speedy that the townspeople below only saw a greenish-orange blur. As he dipped low over a small town, he let loose a stream of fire from his mighty dragon throat. The fairies barely caught a glimpse of what he was aiming for, but it looked like a long row of large clay pots.

Élan giggled a bit as they again rose above the clouds. The fairies were amused to hear dragon giggles as Élan explained, "They make terra cotta pots there. Usually, the pots dry out in the sun for several days, sometimes weeks even, depending on their size. I like to help out with the drying when I pass by, especially this time of year when it's not quite as hot as summer. The pots will be dry and ready for market much sooner."

The fairies smiled, thinking how useful it was for the people in that town to have a dragon for a friend.

After about fifteen minutes, the fairies saw a gigantic lake ahead in the distance. Élan was descending. Before they reached the lake, the fairies caught sight of the first foe. It was a terrible monster indeed. Élan told them, "This is the first of my challenges—a hydra."

Quickly, Snapdragon looked up hydra in her handbook and read aloud to the others:

"*Hydra: A hydra is an enormous monster with nine serpent heads. Hydras are very dangerous, not only because the nine snakeheads are much larger than regular snakeheads; but also, the heads do not tend to get along with each other. This makes the hydra temperamental and in a bad mood most of the time. It does no good to cut off a hydra's head because two more will grow in its place; and this will make the hydra even more miserable and cranky in the long run, with more arguing heads to deal with."*

Élan told Dove and Madam Swallowtail to stay far away from the hydra, and allow Snapdragon and himself to take care of matters initially. Dove and Madam Swallowtail left the security of Élan's crest and dropped behind to give Snapdragon and Élan plenty of room to work. Snapdragon also left the dragon's head and hovered beside Élan, though some distance away to give them both room to maneuver safely.

The hydra was halfway submerged in the center of the lake, and was anything but pleased to see the intruders. Each of the nine heads lunged at Élan and Snapdragon, who dodged the advances very easily. The hydra could not fly, but its huge snake body did rise out of the water very high. As the serpent heads continued to strike, the dragon and fairy continued to evade. Very quickly, both Snapdragon and Élan became speeding blurs.

Élan told Snapdragon, "We'll just wear him out a bit, then maybe he'll talk to us."

The lunges continued, but Snapdragon and Élan were tireless. In fact, both were having great fun: dodging, spinning, whirling, and zooming around to avoid being struck by the hydra's many fangs.

Finally, after nearly twenty minutes, several of the heads began to tire and talk amongst themselves.

"Wait a minute!"

"They don't seem to be giving up."

"Who are they?"

"Stop! What do they want?"

"I'm getting tired of this."

"We better talk to them."

As the nine heads finally stopped lunging, the largest head took the initiative to speak to Élan and Snapdragon. "We want you to leave," it said. "What do you want here?"

Élan politely answered, "I need to cross over your lake on a special quest for my queen."

"No way!" hissed the head, venomously. "No one crosses over our lake!"

Dove had moved a little closer to Élan and Snapdragon, and she called to them. "Ask him if there is anything we could do for him, or get for him, to change his mind."

The hydra heard her suggestion and responded. "Yes, yes, that would be acceptable—some kind of payment."

"What would you like?" asked Snapdragon.

In response to her question, the serpent heads began arguing amongst themselves furiously.

54

"I want ice cream."

"I would like to start a stamp collection."

"A boatload of watermelons."

"We could use some mosquito spray."

"What about satellite television?"

After several minutes of discussion, the heads at last agreed, and the largest head made the request. "We would like music. We all agree that we like music. If you bring us music, we will let you cross over the lake."

Élan was very excited that there was a peaceful solution to this problem, and he quickly told the fairies, "I'll be right back."

As Élan left with a blast of hot air, the three tiny fairies were left hovering over the hydra and immense lake. They didn't have long to worry about the dragon's absence because he was gone less than a minute. Returning with a *whoosh*, Élan swooped down close to the hydra and presented the largest head

with a beautiful, mammoth seashell. The glistening shell was a light purple color, and the fairies could hear enchanting music coming from it.

The dragon returned to the fairies and explained, "A witch, who is a very good friend of mine, lives near here. She was able to quickly enchant the shell to play music forever. That should satisfy the hydra."

Looking below them, the fairies could see that the hydra was indeed very pleased. The long serpent necks were swaying rhythmically to the tempo of the mesmerizing music, as though they were performing a slow, graceful water dance.

Chapter Five

Variant Catifficum

The fairies again came to land on Élan's head to continue their journey. However, before they reached the far shores of the massive lake, they passed through several low-hanging clouds, and the tiny fairies got very wet, soaked in fact.

"Bummer," said Dove.

"Yuck," added Madam Swallowtail, as she tried to shake some of the wetness from her large wings, which were extremely heavy with water. The fairies tried not to complain, but they were now very sticky, clammy, and chilly.

Madam Swallowtail attempted to use her wand with a *Ventilation Spell* to dry the young fairies; however, since they were completely drenched, the drying process was taking a long time.

Before too long, Élan realized what the trouble was. With several puffs of warm air from his nostrils, directed backwards, the fairies were first dried, then lightly steamed, then dried again. In less than two minutes, they were back to normal and very comfortable again.

"Thank you!" the fairies called in unison.

"Next we will meet up with Variant Catifficum," Élan told them. So Snapdragon looked up Variant Catifficum in her handbook:

"Variant Catifficum: Variant Catifficum is an evil, despicable being. He is a shapeshifter who

can take any form and be any size, including dangerous forms and massive sizes. Be careful."

The home of this shapeshifting being was an enormous rock mountain. Variant Catifficum came out from behind several giant boulders, as Élan landed on a large rock ledge.

The fairies hovered next to the dragon's head as Élan spoke to the creature. "We are on an important journey and would like to pass over your mountain."

The shapeshifter was not at all friendly. He was a milky gray color and looked like a thin man, made of smoke. Immediately though, he changed into the shape of a huge ogre, as tall as Élan. Then the ogre began throwing large boulders and stones at the dragon and fairies. However, they were all able to dodge the hurling rocks without difficulty.

Variant Catifficum is an evil, despicable being. He is a shapeshifter who can take any form and be any size, including dangerous forms and massive sizes. Be careful.

Next, the shapeshifter took on the form of lightning. He flashed brilliantly and struck out at the fairies and Élan. With their speed, Snapdragon and Élan were easily able to avoid being hit; however, Madam Swallowtail and Dove had to retreat a good distance to be safe.

Zipping and zooming, this way and that, Snapdragon and Élan evaded the fierce bolts of lightning for some time. However, once more the shifting being took on another form—that of a giant spider. The spider jumped and tried to bite Élan and Snapdragon; but again, they were too fast to be harmed.

Soon, with a little puff of gray smoke, the spider turned into a smoking, red brick chimney. The chimney billowed thick black smoke at the dragon and fairies; but fortunately, a healthy mountain breeze carried most of the nasty, choking clouds away.

Then Variant Catifficum became the ogre again. When the ogre got tired of hurling boulders, he changed once more into lightning. Then the lightning turned into the spider. The spider then became the smoking chimney.

On and on this went—ogre, lightning, spider, chimney—again and again.

Eventually, Élan and the fairies began looking questioningly at one another. This was very confusing. Why wasn't the shapeshifter trying out any other shapes, since these four weren't very effective against the dragon and fairies? Finally, Snapdragon called to him and asked, "Mr. Catifficum, why are you only changing into an ogre, lightning, a spider, and a chimney?"

The shapeshifter stopped shifting and again became the smoky gray thin man. He looked at Snapdragon in amazement. No one had ever asked him a question before. They usually just ran at the sight of his magnificent ogre shape. After a short pause, he answered her question. "I know how to change into these four particular things because I have seen pictures of them. I wish I could take on other forms, but I don't know anything else that would be suitable. I would need examples, like pictures, to work from."

Smiling, Élan asked, "If we provide you with some pictures, would you let us pass over your mountain?"

After thinking for a few moments, Mr. Catifficum responded. "Yes, I would agree to that."

Élan winked at the fairies and was gone in an orange-green blur. Again, he returned quickly, before anyone had time to worry. "I'll make amends later for taking these," he said.

The dragon had brought a large stack of fancy magazines, three colorful catalogs, and several thick books, one of which was an *M* encyclopedia. "There is a wonderful section on monsters in there," Élan explained. "You should be able to get a lot of ideas from these."

"Perfect!" answered Mr. Catifficum. "Wonderful!" he added, perusing the stacks of books and magazines.

"Well, we'll leave you now," Élan said.

The shapeshifter responded with a quick, "Okay, bye." Then he sat down next to the stacks of books and magazines and was immediately engrossed. He had several of them open in front of him as Élan and the fairies departed.

"That was brilliant," Dove told Élan.

The dragon blushed at this praise from the Fairy of Peace, as he flew high over the mountain and into the bright blue sky toward the next challenge.

Chapter Six

The Golem

As they flew toward their next obstacle, the fairies ate a light meal of the peanut butter and marshmallow crème sandwiches, raspberries, and lemon jellybeans. They offered to share their treats with Élan.

"Oh, yes. I'd love some," he said, in answer to their query. "Just toss a sandwich out in front of my head," he added. As Snapdragon tossed the tiny sandwich out in front of him, Élan caught it easily in his large dragon mouth. "Mmmm…that marshmallow crème is so light and fluffy," he said.

The fairies smiled at one another. It was hard to believe that a huge dragon could even taste such a small sandwich.

Next, Élan tried a jellybean. "Yummy!" he exclaimed. "Who would have thought lemon jellybeans were *so* lemony?" Dove and Snapdragon giggled.

"We are going to encounter a golem next," Élan told them.

Again, Snapdragon made use of her fairy handbook:

"*Golem:* A golem is a creature constructed to look like a human being. The creature is given life, but is not a human being. A golem may contain life, but it lacks a soul. Most golems are evil. Some of them have command of dark magic and can be very dangerous. Perhaps the most famous example of a golem is Mary Shelley's literary monster—the

Golem

A Golem is a creature constructed to look like a human being. The creature is given life but is not a human being. A Golem may contain life, but it lacks a soul. Most Golems are evil.

creation of Dr. Frankenstein. You will not be able to tell a well-constructed golem from a human being."

Élan and the fairies approached a vast forest and set down in a large clearing. A rundown wooden shack sat in one corner of the clearing, and a small man came out of the shack just as the dragon landed.

The golem was dressed in blue hospital scrubs. And he was evidently a "well-constructed" golem, because the fairies and dragon couldn't tell by looking at him that he wasn't a man.

"Hello," said Snapdragon. "We are on a special odyssey and must pass over your woods to accomplish our goal."

The golem grinned evilly. "I don't think so," he said. "No one passes over or through my woods. Go back, or around, if you think you can."

Next, the golem raised his hand. With a strange word and a flick of one finger, he hurled a terrible curse at the fairies and Élan, and they had to jump quickly out of the way to avoid being hit. The curse struck a large burr oak tree at the far edge of the clearing. The tree toppled instantly with a terrific crash from the force of the evil spell. Evidently, just as the handbook had warned them, this golem did have possession of dark magic.

With another nasty-looking grin, the golem raised his hand again, and another curse was released at Élan and the fairies. Once more, they dodged. For nearly fifteen minutes, the golem continued to throw curses at them, which the fairies and dragon continued to dodge.

By the time the golem took a break from his curse slinging, the far edge of his clearing looked like a war zone. About forty trees in all had been splintered,

exploded, split, or knocked down by the force of his dark curses. However, the fairies and dragon had managed to stay safe.

While the golem was eyeing them even more evilly, contemplating what else he might try to rid his clearing of the unwelcome visitors, Dove took the opportunity to fly forward and address him with the same words that had worked on the hydra. "Is there anything we could do for you," she asked, "or get for you, so that you will change your mind and allow us to pass?"

The golem scrutinized Dove closely. No one had ever offered to do anything for him before, not once in his whole life. He thought for a few moments, then said, "Maybe there is something..." After another pause, he added, "I was created by a mad scientist, and I am supposed to look just like a real man. Even though the

scientist was brilliant and did an exceptional job, he didn't bother to provide me with any decent clothes. All I have are these old hospital scrubs from his laboratory. If I had something nice, like maybe a blue suit, I would feel more like the human man I am supposed to resemble."

The golem paused yet again, reflecting, before he went on. "Unfortunately, the scientist did not live long after he created me so I could not ask him for proper clothes. You see, though he was a talented craftsman, very gifted with his inventions, he was also crazy. He thought he could fly and jumped off a cliff. Very unfortunate," the golem added, shaking his head sadly.

Élan and the fairies were sad to hear about the death of the golem's creator, but they had to smile. All they needed was a blue suit to solve this problem. Élan told his friends, "I'll be right back."

The fairies and the golem waited patiently. In less than five minutes, Élan returned with a beautiful dark blue suit. He told them, "I left a gold coin on the ground next to the store manikin I took this from."

Next, the golem carefully took the suit into his shack to try it on. When he opened the door, wearing the suit, he was beaming with pride and pleasure. "I love it!" he said.

The pants of the suit were a little long, so Élan immediately pulled a small sewing kit out of thin air, and began hemming the pants to the correct length for the golem. Both the fairies and the golem were very surprised. Who would have thought that dragons were also skilled tailors?

When the pants were hemmed just right, Élan and the fairies stood back to admire. The golem was all smiles as they praised him.

And Snapdragon proclaimed, "Well, you looked like a handsome man before the suit. Now you look like a handsome man, handsomely dressed."

As Élan and the fairies took off, the golem waved and called to them from below. "Good luck with the rest of your journey!"

Chapter Seven

The Chimera

ithin five minutes, they had passed over the far borders of the forest and were flying high over an ocean expanse. Élan told them as he flew, "Our final challenge is to get past a chimera who guards the entrance to the cave where the jewel is located."

Snapdragon was excited to hear this. She remembered several of her friends telling her about their encounter with a chimera on the Island of Shadows the previous year. However, none of the fairies on *this* mission had ever seen a chimera before. She looked up the entry in her handbook and read aloud once more to her fellow fairies:

"Chimera: A chimera is an evil, grotesque, fire-breathing monster made up of two or more different creatures. In the traditional form, a chimera will have the head of a lion, the body of a goat, and the tail of a snake. Chimeras are extremely dangerous. Be careful."

It didn't take long for Élan to cross the ocean. In less than ten minutes, they were soaring right up to a rocky hillside. Élan landed in front of a massive cave opening in the side of the hill.

Just like the hydra, Variant Catifficum, and the golem, the chimera did not take kindly to visitors. Before Élan or the fairies even saw him, they heard a tremendous roar that shook the hillside. The cry of the

Chimera

A Chimera is an evil, grotesque fire-breathing monster made up of two or more different creatures. In the traditional form, a chimera will have the head of a lion, the body of a goat, and the tail of a snake. Chimeras are extremely dangerous. Be careful.

chimera was so loud that it started a small avalanche of dirt and rocks, which poured down the side of the rocky hill. Élan and the fairies rose to hover high above the rockslide until it stopped completely.

The fairies were frightened at their first sight of the chimera as he lumbered out of his cave. This chimera *was* in the traditional form, with a lion's head, a goat's body, and a serpent's tail. His large head was shaggy with dark brown lion's mane, and his goat body was covered with brown and gray streaks. The chimera had two goat legs with huge feet and enormous goat hooves. He also had two small arms sporting hooves that looked as though they couldn't possibly have belonged to such a large creature. The monster's tail was very thick near the body, but tapered off to a point at the tip. The tail was a speckled red and brown color, and it reminded the fairies of a dinosaur's tail.

The chimera was oddly shaped and strangely out of proportion, and it seemed that the tail was needed to steady the monster on his two feet, almost like a tripod.

Right away, the chimera began spitting fireballs at the dragon and fairies. Again, Madam Swallowtail and Dove had to retreat. But Snapdragon and Élan were able to easily dodge the searing balls of fire. This shower of fireballs continued for quite some time, and the chimera seemed to have more energy than the hydra.

It was getting somewhat late in the afternoon, and since Élan needed to complete his quest before nightfall, he told the fairies, "Don't worry, this won't hurt the chimera. I just want to get his attention." Then he added to Snapdragon, "Please fly back a little so you are well out of the way."

As soon as Snapdragon was clear of his field, Élan let loose an intense stream of fire from his enormous mouth. Élan's fire made

the chimera's fireballs look like tiny sparks in comparison. The massive flow of fire was directed at the chimera, but Élan had been right—the chimera was not harmed.

When Élan finally ceased his fiery assault, the chimera looked very mad. And the horrible beast snorted and grunted, thinking, *Show off!* The huge lion mouth roared once again, then fell sulkily silent. However, the chimera did not move from the entrance of the cave. Instead, he eyed Élan and the fairies warily, flicking clouds of dirt and pebbles at them with his giant hooves.

Snapdragon approached and asked the chimera, "Would you please let us into the cave? The dragon is on an important errand for his queen."

The chimera shook his head. He hadn't much liked being showed up by the blast of fire from the dragon. Dragons were supposed to breathe fire. So what if the dragon's fire was more powerful than his! That wasn't going to make him let anyone into his cave.

The chimera knew full well that Élan wanted one of the many jewels secreted in the cave. He had dealt with dragons before. The chimera also knew that dragon fire couldn't hurt him. Élan would have to actually rumble with him, and physically overpower him, to gain entrance to the cave. The chimera was slightly larger than the dragon, and a scrapple with another monster his size was probably going to be a pretty even match.

However, hoping for a peaceful solution, Élan stepped forward and told the chimera, "I'm sorry about the blast of fire, but we wanted to speak with you. We would be willing to give you something in exchange for entrance to the cave. What would you like? Just name it, and I will try to get it for you."

The chimera looked at Élan and the fairies rather suspiciously. The last dragon that came for a jewel had mixed things up with him and had knocked him down the hill before going into the cave to take one of the jewels. The chimera found it hard to believe that *this* dragon was willing to give him a gift to gain entrance to the cave.

The creature thought about this proposal for some time before answering. Finally, the chimera thought that it was worth the shot to ask for something. It couldn't hurt, in case the dragon was serious; and the chimera had heard somewhere that dragons were supposed to be honest and truthful.

"I am kind of hungry," the chimera told them. "I would like some bananas. They are my favorite food, and I can't go off to find them because I have to stay here to guard the cave. But if you bring me some bananas, I will let you in."

This time, Élan was gone and back so fast that the fairies weren't even sure he had actually left. But he had piles of bananas on his back and was carrying several bunches in his front claws. The chimera was over-joyed. "What a feast!" he exclaimed. "My favorite food," he said grate-fully. Then the chimera added, "I also have a toothache, which is why I am cranky most of the time. But I don't suppose you can do anything about that," he said dejectedly, shaking his shaggy head.

Élan smiled, and with a click of his claws, a green spark appeared near his nose. The spark then turned into a tiny green cloud that moved forward and entered the mouth of the chimera who was instantly healed of his toothache pain.

"Wow! Thank you!" the chimera said earnestly.

Then Élan told the chimera, "Since I know that you like bananas, I will bring you some whenever I pass this way." The fairies almost thought they saw tears in the chimera's large brown eyes.

As the chimera settled himself in for a banana smorgasbord, Élan and the fairies made their way to the mouth of the cave.

Upon entering the cave, the fairies were overwhelmed by the massive cache of jewels contained in the enormous chamber. Élan explained to them, "This is a hoard that used to belong to an evil giant king." There were mounds of sparkling jewels everywhere in the trove, and many of them were larger than basketballs. One ruby was even the size of a beach ball. There was also a pile of lustrous black pearls, each the size of a large grapefruit.

Élan knew exactly what he was looking for. From one corner of the cave, he selected a square-shaped peridot that was about the size of large shoebox. He told the fairies, "Queen Elektra told me she would like something green, but she already has several emeralds. This will go perfectly with her eyes."

As they were leaving the cave, the fairies gave one more look over their shoulders at the heaps of jewels. The multitudes of enormous sapphires, pearls, diamonds, and other precious stones were something they would never forget; but they wanted to have a last glance. Then they said goodbye to the chimera, who was still happily munching on bananas, and set off to deliver the jewel to Queen Elektra.

Chapter Eight

Queen Elektra

The dragon colony was located in a secret place in the mountains. Élan flew very high above the clouds, as was tradition when bringing any visitors to a dragon colony, so that no one could recognize the landscape and return. However, the ground was whizzing by so fast, the fairies would never have been able to commit the geography to memory anyway.

When Élan landed, high on a secluded mountaintop, several, obviously older dragons surrounded them. The fairies assumed that the other dragons were older because they were larger than Élan. The monstrous creatures were many different colors, mostly very bright shades of purple, green, red, pink, lilac, and orange. Many of them welcomed Élan with pats on the back, and some let loose jets of fire and steam in throaty congratulations.

Queen Elektra herself was nearly twice the size of Élan. None of the fairies would have ever imagined that a dragon could be as large as a two-story building. Queen Elektra was a brilliant shade of electric blue, and she had yellowy-green, piercing eyes.

The queen welcomed Élan and the fairies kindly.

"Hello! I'm glad you have returned safely," she said to Élan. The queen's voice was very much like Élan's, low and gentle, but there was a ladylike quality to it. "Welcome, fairies! We don't have many fairy visitors to our colony."

Élan approached his queen respectfully, presenting her with the jewel.

"Oh, magnificent," she breathed. "Perfectly lovely." Then, in a louder, more ceremonial voice, she announced, "Élan, we are pleased to welcome you into dragon adulthood!" With this statement, Queen Elektra presented Élan with a magnificent silver toe ring that had an intricately carved design of leaves and vines. The design was imbedded with blue stones that perfectly matched Élan's eyes. Élan blushed furiously for a moment, then slipped the ring onto the third toe of his left back foot. The fairies noticed that the older dragons all wore toe rings on their left back feet too.

Next, Élan circled around the dragon gathering, introducing the fairies to many of his dragon friends. The fairies were pleased to meet the dragons. It was obvious that most of them were indeed as peaceful as Élan.

As it was getting dark, the fairies were invited to join the feast celebration for Élan's successful completion of the Rites of Dragondom. The delicious spread included piles of mangos, mounds of chocolate covered glazed donuts, tubs of strawberry pudding, heaps of salt water taffy, dozens of bubble-gum-flavored chiffon cakes, stacks of black licorice, and huge platters of baked Alaska.

When the tiny fairies were stuffed very full of the sweets, and were starting to get sleepy, Élan suggested that it was time for him to fly them home.

The return journey took less than an hour.

Élan dropped Dove off first, at the state park campsite. Periwinkle, Cinnabar, and Madam June Beetle had been waiting anxiously for her to arrive. What an exciting campfire tale Dove was able to share with her friends.

Snapdragon and Madam Swallowtail were dropped off at Madam Swallowtail's home. Luna and Madam Finch were waiting up for them. They had pepperoni pizza, salad, and root beer all ready to go as a late-night supper for their tired friends. However, Snapdragon and Madam Swallowtail couldn't even manage two bites because they were still quite full from the dragon sweet feast. But it was nice to sit and sip root beer, and share the adventure with their friends.

Snapdragon and Dove spent the last of their spring vacation resting and sending nut messages to their friends, telling them of the success of their exciting mission.

A week later, they both received nut messages from Élan, thanking them for helping him complete his peaceful odyssey. Included with each note was a tiny silver toe ring, identical to the one Élan had received from his queen. The girls were very excited to receive the beautiful gifts.

Snapdragon decided to wear her ring on her finger, instead of her toe. Some girls at school wore toe rings, but Snapdragon liked finger rings better.

Dove decided to wear her ring on a silver chain around her neck. She did a lot of crafts such as pottery and basketry. Since she was so busy with her hands, and got them messy a lot, she didn't wear jewelry very often. Wearing the ring as a pendant meant that she could have the treasured keepsake near her, but it would not get dirty or messed up while working on projects.

Élan was happily accepted into the dragon colony with full rights, his place secure for all eternity.

Queen Elektra loved the beautiful peridot he had obtained for her. She wore it proudly around her neck. The gem

really did look magnificent with her gleaming green eyes.

However, there was another, rather odd outcome to Élan's odyssey. Wherever he went, doves followed him. And he was often seen with rows of doves perched on his wings and his head. Sometimes, hundreds of doves would gather around him, cooing softly, bringing him good dreams and telling him about their travels. And they seemed to like to fly with him whenever they could manage to keep up.

This didn't bother Élan. He liked his new friends. Even when some of his fellow dragons started calling him Deedee, which was short for Dovedragon, Élan didn't mind because he thought it was a good idea to have birds, and fairies, as friends.

The End

Fairy Fun

Clay Pot:

Élan the dragon likes to help pottery dry by heating it with his flames. But here's a recipe for clay you can use that doesn't need a dragon's fire to dry. Be sure to get an adult's permission before you start.

You will need:
  2 ½ cups flour
  1 cup water
  1 cup salt
  Food coloring (optional)

Mix all of the ingredients in a large bowl. Add a drop or two of food coloring if you'd like. Once the dough is well combined, shape it into whatever you would like. Try making a vase, or roll it out flat and cut out a shape with a cookie cutter. When you have a shape that you like, place it on a piece of waxed paper and let dry for 48 hours. Once the shape is completely dried, you can paint it or leave it its natural color.

Keep the Earth Clean

Snapdragon's Girls Club adopted a section of a highway to regularly clean up litter. You can help Snapdragon keep our planet clean by picking up litter too.

Check with your local kids' organizations (such as Girl Scouts) to see if they have cleanup projects you can help with. Ask your teachers if you can create a cleaning team to help keep your school's playgrounds free from litter. If you belong to a church, synagogue, mosque, or any other type of organization, see if there are others who would like to help you round up litter from playgrounds, the shores of ponds

and lakes, forest preserves, and anywhere else you can think of. The more people who get involved, the easier (and more fun) it will be.

Even if you cannot form a group to help pick up litter, keep an eye out for it in your own yard or wherever you are. If you notice an empty can on the ground, recycle it. If someone has left a newspaper on a park bench, recycle it. Of course, you should always practice safety when picking up things from the ground. Watch out for broken glass or sharp objects. When in doubt, ask a grown-up first!

Animal Camouflage

Many animals (like chameleons) use camouflage to protect themselves from predators. Their fur, skin, or scales have colors and patterns similar to the environment in which they live. For example, snowshoe hares live in cold, snowy climates, so their fur is pure white to help them blend in with the snow around them. Many owls (such as the boreal owl) and other birds, fish, frogs, insects (like the walking stick insect), and toads have appearances that make them almost invisible to predators. Arctic foxes have fur that changes color depending on the season—reddish brown in the warm months to help them hide in forests and white in the winter to blend with snow.

Some animals and insects have disguises that make their predators afraid of them. The owl butterfly has two large eyespots on its wings.

When it is resting, a predator will see the eyes and think something huge is staring back at it. Other animals use camouflage in order to catch their prey. That's right, predators have camouflage too! The African lion's fur is the same tawny shade of brown as the tall grasses in the desert, making them hard for their prey to see. An alligator's dark, bumpy skin lets it hide in marshes, nearly invisible to its prey until it attacks.

Bamboo

There are many different species of bamboo plants; some can grow over 100 feet tall! Because of its tall sizes and wide variety of uses, you may not know that bamboo is actually a type of grass. It grows in many different parts of the world, including Asia, Australia, Africa, and even parts of North and South America.

Bamboo can be used for many different purposes. Tall bamboo can be used for building and construction. Many buildings in Asia feature bamboo poles and furniture made out of bamboo. Bamboo scaffolding is used by construction workers when working on tall buildings. Panda bears eat bamboo shoots as part of their regular diet. Evan humans eat bamboo shoots in different types of food. Bamboo can also be made into yarn, paper, knitting needles, musical instruments, chopsticks, and much more.

After being harvested, bamboo can grow back very rapidly. Some types of bamboo can grow 3 to 4 feet a day! Bamboo can be harvested every 3 to 5 years, whereas it can take 10 to 20 years to grow a new tree after it has been cut down for lumber. This speedy growth rate makes bamboo a wonderful renewable resource. (A renewable resource is something that can grow back after it has been used.)

Inside you is the power to do anything™

. . . the adventures continue

Luna and the Well of Secrets

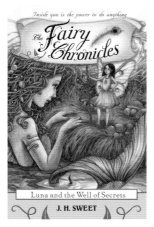

Luna and the Well of Secrets

J. H. SWEET

Three bat fairies have been kidnapped and taken to the Well of Secrets. To make matters worse, the Well of Secrets is the doorway to Eventide, the Land of Darkness!

"There must be extremely powerful magic involved to snatch fairies from three completely different parts of the world all in one day."

Madam Toad's face wore a puzzled expression as she continued. "And the reason only bat fairies were abducted is unknown..."

Luna, Snapdragon, Firefly, and Madam Finch are sent to the Well to discover why. Once there, they discover a Dark Witch imprisoned in a mirror, only able to come out for twelve minutes every twelve hours. Then a Light Witch arrives and the fairies have to make a choice. Who do they trust? Which one is good and which one is evil? Will they defeat the right witch without destroying the balance between light and dark?

This may be the most dangerous fairy mission ever!

Come visit us at fairychronicles.com

Dewberry and the Lost Chest of Paragon

Dewberry and the Lost Chest of Paragon

J. H. SWEET

In Dewberry's constant quest to obtain more knowledge, she uncovers the Legend of Paragon, an ancient ruler, and his three marshals— Exemplar, Criterion, and Apotheosis. Dewberry enlists the aid of her friends, Primrose and Snapdragon, in seeking the Lost Chest of Paragon, rumored to contain a great gift of ancient and powerful knowledge, one she hopes to share with all of mankind.

"Maybe it's a cure for cancer," suggested Primrose.

"Or diabetes, or epilepsy, or cystic fibrosis," added Snapdragon hopefully.

Primrose had another idea. "Maybe it's a blueprint for World Peace," she said.

The girls were very excited about the many possibilities.

But when the chest is found, a catastrophe occurs, one so powerful that even fairy magic is nowhere near strong enough to fix the problem. But it was Dewberry's relentless search for knowledge that caused this disaster in the first place. She will have to do everything she can to make it right again...

Come visit us at fairychronicles.com

Moonflower and the Pearl of Paramour

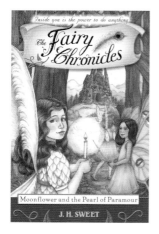

Henry, a brownie prince, loves the fairy named Rose. Forty years ago, a bitter wizard cursed them to be forever apart and forever silent. Rose is trapped in a magic painting and Henry is trapped in a book. Neither can leave their prisons, nor speak a single word, or the other will die.

But every seventy-two years, the Wishing Star of Love appears for nine days only, and when wished upon, it can lead the wisher to Paramour, the Goddess of Love. With the help of the Goddess's magic pearl, there is a way to set the cursed couple free. Since Moonflower is the Fairy of Love, she will lead the mission to rescue Henry and Rose. Can

Moonflower and her friends reach Henry and Rose in time or will the couple be imprisoned forever?

Come visit us at fairychronicles.com

The adventures don't end here!

Come visit us at
www.fairychronicles.com

for even more fairy magic and fun!

- Become a Fairy Chronicles member
- Upload your own fairy drawings
- Read about all of the *Fairy Chronicles* adventures—and get sneak peeks of the next books
- Meet each fairy and learn more about your favorite characters
- Help protect Mother Nature with cool recycling activities and ideas
- Check out the online Fairy Handbook as well as trivia, recipes, poems, and crafts
- Download special bookmarks, computer graphics, and more free stuff
- Send your friends *Fairy Chronicles* e-cards

And much more!

About the Author

J. H. Sweet has always looked for the magic in the everyday. She has an imaginary dog named Jellybean Ebenezer Beast. Her hobbies include hiking, photography, knitting, and basketry. She also enjoys watching a variety of movies and sports. Her favorite superhero is her husband, with Silver Surfer coming in a close second. She loves many of the same things the fairies love, including live oak trees, mockingbirds, weathered terra-cotta, butterflies, bees, and cypress knees. In the fairy game of "If I were a jellybean, what flavor would I be?" she would be green apple. J. H. Sweet lives with her husband in South Texas and has a degree in English from Texas State University.

About the Illustrator

Holly Sierra's illustrations are visually enchanting with particular attention to decorative, mystical, and multicultural themes. Holly received her fine arts education at SUNY Purchase in New York and lives in Myrtle Beach with her husband, Steve, and their three children, Gabrielle, Esme, and Christopher.